Now
Winky Blue!

by Pamela Jane
illustrated by
G. Brian Karas

For Kassie, Teddy, Maggie, and Kip,
And the real Winky Blue–P.J.

For Emelia–G.B.K.

For information contact:
MONDO Publishing
980 Avenue of the Americas
New York, New York 10018
Visit our website at www.mondopub.com

Printed in Canada
June, 2011, Webcom, Inc. (Toronto, Canada), Co. Ltd - 377559

11 12 13 14   12 11 10 9

Design by Roberta Pressel

Library of Congress Cataloging-in-Publication Data
Jane, Pamela.
    No way, Winky Blue! / by Pamela Jane ; illustrated by G. Brian Karas.
      p.   cm.
    Summary: In her search for a great pet Rosie finally decides upon a parakeet, but when it fails to meet her expectations, she is disappointed.
    ISBN 1-57255-238-7 (pbk.)
    [1. Parakeets–Fiction. 2. Pets–Fiction.]   I. Karas, G. Brian, ill. II. Title.
PZ7.J213Nm   1996
[Fic]–dc20   95-53367
                                                  CIP
                                                  AC

Contents

Hello, Winky Blue!

Rosie closed her eyes and took a deep breath. She did that every time she visited Wags 'n' Whiskers Pet Shop.

Michael poked her.

"Rosie, what are you *doing?*"

"I'm smelling," said Rosie, breathing deeply.

Rosie loved the way the pet shop smelled of warm puppies, and dog biscuits, and squeaky rubber toys. The smell made her happy.

Michael giggled. "You look funny," he said.

Rosie opened her eyes. Her happy feeling went away. The puppies were there, all right. But seeing them made her sad.

Ever since she had gone to see the movie *Lassie,* Rosie had longed for a smart, brave dog, one who could do tricks and rescue people from danger. But Rosie's Aunt Maria said their house was too small for a dog.

And that was a *big* problem.

Rosie sighed. Michael understood how she felt.

"Maybe your Aunt Maria will let you get something else, like a spider," he said. "My sister Karen had a pet tarantula that was real friendly."

Rosie giggled. "No way am I getting anything with long, hairy legs, Michael!"

"Lassie has long, hairy legs," Michael pointed out.

"That's different," said Rosie. "Lassie can jump fences and attack crooks."

"How about a gerbil?" suggested Michael. "They don't take up much room."

Rosie shook her head. "Can you see a gerbil attacking a crook?"

Michael grew quiet. Rosie knew he was thinking hard. She waited hopefully. If there was anyone who could help solve her problem, it was Michael.

"I know!" said Michael. "You could get a parakeet. They're small, and they don't have hairy legs."

Rosie looked doubtful. "Can parakeets do tricks and warn people of danger, like Lassie?" she asked.

"I'm not sure," said Michael. "You can teach them to talk, though. Even Lassie can't do that."

Rosie and Michael walked over to a big cage filled with brightly-colored parakeets. One was asleep with its head under its wing. Another hopped back and forth, chattering to itself in the mirror.

Rosie peered curiously at them. "They don't look too smart," she said.

Just then one of the parakeets hopped right over to where Rosie stood. His breast was a soft blue, the color of a robin's egg. He cocked his head and winked his bright black eyes at Rosie.

Rosie smiled. "Hello, Winky," she said softly. "Hello, Winky Blue."

Michael looked surprised. "Why did you call him Winky Blue?"

"Because he winked at me," said Rosie, "and he's blue, the color of a robin's egg."

The blue parakeet winked and nodded, as though he understood perfectly. Then he held out his claw to Rosie.

"Look, he wants to shake hands!" cried Rosie. "Michael, this bird is really smart. With a little training, Winky Blue could be a star, like Lassie."

Michael grinned. "All you have to do now is talk your Aunt Maria into letting you get him."

A Good Luck Sign

Mrs. Humphrey, Michael's mother, was waiting for Rosie and Michael outside, in the car. On the drive home, Michael and Rosie whispered together in the back seat. They could whisper loudly because Lily, Michael's baby sister, was making a big racket banging her rattle against her car seat.

"Please, *please,* let Aunt Maria say yes," Rosie whispered, crossing her fingers for luck.

Michael crossed his fingers, too.

"Parakeets don't take up much space," he said. "You could keep Winky's cage right in your room."

"And I have enough money to buy him all by myself," added Rosie.

Mr. Blackwell, the pet store owner, said parakeets cost fifteen dollars. Rosie had exactly sixteen dollars and sixty-seven cents saved up from her allowance and the money the tooth fairy had left under her pillow.

"You'll have to buy a birdcage," said Michael.

"Uh-oh!" said Rosie. "I forgot about that. I don't have enough money for a cage."

Mrs. Humphrey stopped at a red light.

"What are you two whispering about back there?" she asked, turning around.

"Nothing!" answered Rosie and Michael at the same time. Michael's mother was friends with Rosie's aunt, so they had to be careful about what they said.

"Michael, I have to get the money for a cage before someone else buys my bird," Rosie whispered when the car started again.

Michael was quiet for a minute. Then suddenly he brightened. "If I had a loose tooth, and if I yanked it out, I might get a dollar from the tooth fairy."

Rosie shook her head. "I don't want you pulling any teeth for me," she said. "Besides, birdcages cost a lot. We'll have to think of something else."

Mrs. Humphrey pulled up in front of Rosie's house. Next door, Mrs. Bupp was having a yard sale before she moved away.

Mrs. Bupp's front yard was littered with cast-off clothes, old tools, and worn-out furniture. Lionel, the stray tabby cat, was stretched out on a faded patchwork quilt.

"There's a pet you could have for free," said Michael, pointing to Lionel.

Rosie laughed. "No way!" she said. "Lionel's too mean looking."

"Well, what do you want for free?" said Michael. But Rosie was right. Lionel wasn't at all cute or cuddly. He had a bald tail from a fight with a dog (the dog lost) and a nasty look in his eye. The old cat didn't belong to anyone, but Mrs. Bupp always fed him leftovers, so Lionel hung around, waiting for more. Today, however, Mrs. Bupp was too busy with her yard sale to think about Lionel.

"I bet most of her stuff isn't worth much," said Rosie. Then something caught her eye.

"Do you see what I see?" she whispered, grabbing Michael's arm.

Michael nodded, his eyes wide.

Sitting on a table in Mrs. Bupp's front yard was a birdcage. And on the cage was a big tag that said $1.50.

"It's a good luck sign," whispered Rosie, "a sign that Winky Blue is meant to be mine!"

Rosie's Promise

"Now don't forget," whispered Michael before Rosie got out of the car, "wait for the right moment to ask about Winky, slow down, and stay calm."

"Just leave everything to me," said Rosie.

Rosie found her aunt in the dining room writing her "Ask Aunt Maria" column for the local newspaper. Every week, high school girls wrote to Aunt Maria to ask advice about their boy problems.

When Rosie saw Aunt Maria, her heart started beating hard and her head felt funny. She took a deep breath.

Wait for the right moment, she reminded herself. Slow down, and stay calm.

"He's small and I can keep him in my room and Michael won't have to pull any teeth because Mrs. Bupp has a cage for a dollar fifty!" Rosie blurted out.

Aunt Maria looked up from her computer, surprised. Rosie was surprised herself. She hadn't meant to blurt everything out. And she wasn't finished yet.

"And I love him!" Rosie added.

"Don't tell me you have a boy problem," said Aunt Maria.

"He is a boy," said Rosie. "A boy parakeet. He's at Wags 'n' Whiskers and he's meant to be mine."

"Now Rosie, slow down and start from the beginning," said Aunt Maria. "What is it about this bird that's so special?"

Rosie sat down and started again. This time she remembered to stay calm and talk slowly.

"Winky Blue is smart," she began. "I'm sure

of that. He's brave, too, I can tell. And loyal. We can have exciting adventures together, like in *Lassie*."

"Go on," said Aunt Maria.

Rosie's heart lifted. Aunt Maria hadn't said yes, but she hadn't said no, either.

"Our house is big enough for a parakeet," Rosie went on. "Look at all the room we have," she said, spreading her arms wide.

Ever since she could remember, Rosie had lived with her Aunt Maria. First they'd lived in a tiny apartment. It had been Rosie's parents' apartment before they'd died in a plane accident, when Rosie was a baby.

Rosie had been happy living in the apartment with Aunt Maria and seventeen stuffed animals (no live pets were allowed). But then, over the summer, something wonderful had happened. Rosie and her aunt had moved to their own house. The house had two bedrooms, a basement, and a yard. To Rosie it didn't seem a bit small. It seemed like a mansion.

"I'll take care of Winky all by myself," said Rosie. "He won't be any trouble. I promise, Aunt Maria."

Aunt Maria tapped her long fingernails on the table.

"Parakeets can live a long time," she said. "How will you feel about taking care of this bird when you're a teenager?"

"I'll love Winky Blue forever!" said Rosie, her eyes shining.

"I know teenagers," said Aunt Maria, glancing at the stack of letters beside her computer. "You'll be more interested in clothes and boys when you're in high school. You'll forget all about Winky."

"I'll never forget Winky," said Rosie. "Oh, Aunt Maria, if you could only see him, you'd understand."

"Well," said Aunt Maria, "taking care of any pet is a lot of work. Are you sure you want to do it?"

"I'm positive." said Rosie.

"And you won't forget to feed him and change his cage?"

"No way!"

"I'll tell you what, Rosie," said Aunt Maria. "I'm going to leave this up to you. If you really think..."

Rosie didn't hear the rest. She was already racing down the hall to get her piggy bank.

Winky's Magic Adventure

"Isn't he beautiful?" Rosie said it again. "Isn't he beautiful?"

"He *is* cute," said Michael.

"And smart. Winky's going to be a great hero," said Rosie confidently.

Winky cocked his head and winked at Rosie. He seemed to like his new home, in his cage in Rosie's room.

"Michael, look!" said Rosie. "Winky's breathing." Rosie watched Winky's soft blue breast rise and fall as he breathed in and out.

"Sure he's breathing," said Michael. "He's

alive."

"And he's all mine!" said Rosie with a long, happy sigh. Rosie loved her stuffed animals, but this was different. Winky was a real, living bird, and he belonged just to her.

"Uh-oh," she said, reaching into Winky's cage. "Time to change his water dish."

"That's the third time you've changed it since we got home," said Michael.

Rosie smiled. "I have to take good care of Winky. It's up to me to make sure he has a wonderful life."

Suddenly Rosie had an idea.

"Michael, let's make Winky a magical place, all shiny and beautiful. A place fit for a star."

"Like Magic Adventure," said Michael. Magic Adventure was a new amusement park on Silver Lake, up north. Michael and Rosie had seen pictures of it in a magazine.

Rosie nodded. "We can use my mirror for the lake."

Michael helped set Rosie's wall mirror down on the bedroom floor. A beam of sunlight dancing through the trees rippled across the silvery surface.

"Look, Winky," said Rosie, "your very own lake!"

"Footzwinkly," chattered Winky, hopping back and forth on his perch. "Pottsfitz!"

"What are we going to do for rides?" asked Rosie. "Magic Adventure has a roller coaster and a Ferris wheel."

"My baby sister has a toy Ferris wheel," said Michael. "We can borrow that."

As it turned out, the Ferris wheel was too small for Winky to ride in. So Rosie and Michael filled the tiny cars with bird seed and set it on the mirror. Then Rosie carried Winky gently to the shining new land they had made for him.

Winky sat on the mirror, blinking his bright black eyes at the splendor around him.

"Look, he loves it," whispered Rosie. "No

way will Winky want to go back to his cage after this."

Winky fluffed out his feathers and pecked at his image in the mirror. Then he pecked at the bright Ferris wheel, making it turn slowly around. Michael and Rosie laughed.

Rosie felt proud and happy to be in charge of Winky's life, and his future. She got up three times during the night, just to make sure he was all right. Each time Winky was sleeping soundly under his birdcage cover. Finally, Rosie fell asleep and dreamed of a magical land with a brightly-colored Ferris wheel and a shining lake. And in the middle of all this was a treasure, something warm and real and alive.

Winky Blue.

28

Big Plans

"Today," Rosie announced when Michael came over the next morning, "we're going to start having adventures with Winky. We'll start by teaching him tricks."

"Squawk!" cried Winky, hopping back and forth excitedly. He was ready.

Michael nodded. "My uncle Joe had a canary that could shake hands with its foot."

"That's too easy," said Rosie. "Any bird can do that."

Rosie picked up the cassette tape Mrs. Bupp had given her free, with the bird cage. Printed on the front, in big letters, were the magic words "Teach Your Parakeet to Talk!"

"We're going to teach Winky Blue to talk," said Rosie. "No way can Lassie do that!"

Rosie placed her small cassette player on her desk, next to Winky's cage. Then she popped in the tape and pressed the PLAY button.

"Congratulations, boys and girls!" boomed a man's deep voice. "You have taken the first step in teaching your parakeet to talk."

"Cheep. Goofunkle!" chattered Winky, hopping back and forth.

"Teaching your parakeet to talk will take a little time," continued the voice, more serious now.

Rosie and Michael looked at each other.

"I hope it doesn't take *too* long," said Rosie. "I want to start having exciting adventures right away."

"I will repeat one phrase over and over so that your parakeet will learn it," the voice on the tape went on. "And now I suggest you leave your pet alone for half an hour so it can pay attention to the lesson."

Winky hopped to the end of his perch and cocked his head, listening to the recording.

"Hello, how are you?" the lesson began.

"Come on," said Michael. "Let's get out of here."

Rosie glanced at her desk clock.

"It's exactly ten o'clock," she whispered. "Winky has until ten thirty to learn his first lesson."

Michael grinned. "When we come back, he'll say, 'Hello, how are you?'"

"And that's just the beginning," said Rosie as they tiptoed away. "I have plans for Winky. Big plans."

Hopes and Dreams

"Is it time yet?" asked Rosie.

"Rosie, it's only been two minutes," said Michael, peering at Aunt Maria's big kitchen clock. "The man on the tape said it would take a half-hour to teach Winky to talk."

Michael went back to the booklet he was reading, *Parakeets of the World*. Aunt Maria had bought it for Rosie, along with bird seed and special paper for Winky's cage.

Rosie swung her legs impatiently under the kitchen table. She didn't care about parakeets of the world. She only cared about Winky Blue. He was the one parakeet who was going to turn her ordinary life into an adventure, like in *Lassie*. Every day would be another exciting episode. And teaching Winky to talk was the first step.

Rosie stared at the big hand on the clock. It seemed to take forever to move one minute. But ten thirty came at last.

"I'm so excited!" whispered Rosie as she opened her bedroom door. She held her breath, waiting to hear Winky's first words.

"Hello, how are you?" a voice greeted them. It was the man on the tape.

"Cheep!" sang Winky when he saw Rosie. "Woofitz-woopstum. Nootfunkle!"

Rosie's face fell. "Michael, Winky hasn't learned one word!"

"Fitzboo!" chattered Winky happily.

"He never said that before," said Michael.

"You know what I mean," said Rosie. "Winky hasn't learned one word of English. He's still talking bird talk. What are we going to do?"

Michael frowned and scratched his head.

"I read that there were two dogs who played Lassie on TV," he said. "We could have two Winkys, and the other one could do all the tricks."

"But I don't have two parakeets," said Rosie. "And all my hopes are pinned on this one."

"Maybe we could teach Winky something else," said Michael, "like carrying urgent messages in his beak."

So Rosie and Michael spent the rest of the morning cutting out little pieces of paper and printing messages on them. Michael wrote, "Help!" and "Fire!" Rosie's said, "A monster is after me!" But all Winky did with the messages was peck at them. He even ate the one that said, "A monster is after me!"

Next, Rosie and Michael tried to teach Winky to dial 9-1-1, in case of an emergency. But Winky couldn't even get a dial tone on Aunt Maria's cordless telephone.

Rosie tried hard to be patient. She took

seven deep breaths. She closed her eyes and counted to ten. After that she counted to twenty-one.

Then she exploded.

"No way is Winky ever going to be a hero!" she cried. "Even if a crook broke into our house, Winky would probably just chirp like he was happy to see him."

"Chirp!" said Winky.

"Oh, be quiet," said Rosie. She grabbed the birdcage cover and threw it over Winky's cage.

Instantly, Winky grew quiet under the dark cover.

"Rosie," said Michael, "it's not Winky's fault he can't learn anything."

"But he acted so smart in the pet store," said Rosie. "Now I get home and he acts dumb."

Rosie's eyes filled with tears. She had staked everything on Winky Blue. Her greatest hopes, her wildest dreams.

And sixteen dollars and fifty cents.

Escape!

"Aunt Maria, I need advice," said Rosie, after Michael left.

Aunt Maria looked up from the newspaper. Every Sunday, Rosie's aunt sat down with a cup of coffee and read her "Ask Aunt Maria" advice column. Aunt Maria loved reading her own advice, and she was always happy to give more.

"No way is Winky ever going to be a hero, or a star," Rosie began. "Michael and I couldn't get him to learn one trick. And I had all these plans. Every day was going to be like a Lassie movie."

"Maybe you set your goals too high," said Aunt Maria, pouring herself a second cup of coffee. "Winky is a fine bird, even if he isn't like Lassie."

Rosie said nothing. She didn't think she had set her goals too high. She'd set them exactly where she wanted them.

"Why don't you forget about turning Winky into a star," suggested Aunt Maria. "Just enjoy him. Have fun."

Rosie nodded and walked slowly back to her room, thinking about Aunt Maria's advice. It was good advice, she knew. Who could argue with having fun?

"Cheep!" said Winky when Rosie came in. He sounded sad and forlorn under his birdcage cover. But Rosie pretended not to hear him.

The truth was, Rosie wasn't ready to take her aunt's advice—yet. Because in one tiny corner of her heart she was still very, very mad.

"Hey, Rosie!" called a voice outside her bedroom window.

Rosie opened the window and leaned out. Michael was standing outside wearing a pair of dark glasses and a purple raincoat that came down past his ankles.

"Look at all this great stuff Mrs. Bupp left out for the thrift store." he called, waving his arms. "She said we could open the boxes as long as we put everything back."

"Wait a second," Rosie called. "I'll be right there."

Rosie grabbed a jacket. Outside, in the warm October sun, she and Michael rummaged through the boxes. They found all sorts of good things–western hats and long capes and belts with big buckles. When they got tired of looking through the boxes, they chased each other around, wearing floppy boots and waving old umbrellas.

"Help, a monster is after me!" shouted Michael.

Lionel, the stray tabby cat, sat on Mrs. Bupp's front porch, glaring as they raced by.

"Kids," he seemed to say. "UGH!"

Rosie and Michael ran until they were red and out of breath. Then they fell down in a pile of leaves, rolling and shouting.

Afterwards, Rosie hurried home, happy and smiling. Running and shouting and laughing had chased away her angry feelings. She felt better about Winky, but she felt worse about the way she had treated him. Aunt Maria was right. Winky was a good bird. He was friendly and cheerful. And he chirped whenever Rosie came into the room. That was sort of a trick.

But there was something more important than that.

Winky is counting on me to take care of him, thought Rosie. *I'm his little girl, the way he's my bird.*

When Rosie got home, she ran straight to her room and uncovered Winky's cage. But this time, Winky didn't chirp. He didn't do anything because he wasn't there. His cage was empty under the birdcage cover.

And Winky was nowhere to be seen.

The Blue Feather

"It's all my fault," cried Rosie. "If I hadn't gotten mad and covered Winky up, I would have seen that I left his cage door open."

"And if I hadn't called for you to come out, you wouldn't have left the window open," said Michael.

"But you did, and Winky must have flown out," said Aunt Maria, gazing out the window with a worried look. Outside, the sun slanted low through the trees, and a cool autumn breeze rustled the leaves.

"Winky will find his way back, I know he will!" said Rosie. She had called Aunt Maria and

Michael as soon as she discovered that Winky was missing.

Michael stared silently at Rosie.

"What is it?" said Rosie. "Michael, tell me!"

"Parakeets can't find their way home by themselves," said Michael. "It says so in your bird book. They die unless someone rescues them."

Rosie started to cry. "I was mean to Winky because he wasn't a super-bird. And now he's gone and he'll never know how much I loved him."

Rosie was crying hard now. "No way will I ever get mad at Winky again, if only he'd come back," she sobbed.

Aunt Maria looked solemn. "We'd better go look for Winky before it gets dark—and cold," she said.

Rosie was already halfway down the hall.

Michael, Rosie, and Aunt Maria looked everywhere for Winky. They looked in treetops, under leaves, and behind woodpiles. Even

Michael's sister, Karen, joined in the search.

"Here, Winky!" they called. "Here, Winky Blue!"

Rosie shouted until she was hoarse, but she heard no answering *chirp!*

What she did hear was a meow.

Lionel came trotting over from next door. He sat down in front of Rosie and started cleaning his face. The old cat looked fat and contented, as though he had just enjoyed a good meal. Then Rosie noticed something that made her knees start to shake. Lionel had a feather stuck to the end of his nose.

And the feather was robin's egg blue.

Empty Cage

Rosie screamed. Michael stared. Aunt Maria turned white.

"He ate him!" yelled Rosie. "That cat ate my bird!"

Lionel stopped cleaning his face and gave Rosie a dirty look as if to say, "So what if I did?"

Rosie started crying again. "Bird killer!" she sobbed. "Murderer!"

Aunt Maria put her arm around her.

"Rosie, I know it's a hard lesson," she said softly.

"I was mean to Winky Blue," sobbed Rosie. "And now he's dead and he'll never know I loved him."

That night, Rosie lay awake for a long time, staring into the moonlight. The bars of Winky's empty cage made eerie shadows against the wall, like skeleton bones.

It was hard to believe. Only yesterday Rosie had been planning all the wonderful adventures she and Winky would have together. Winky was going to be a hero and perform brave and

courageous deeds. But Winky was no star, Rosie admitted to herself. He was a lovable, friendly, ordinary parakeet.

At least he used to be.

No way will I ever get another parakeet, Rosie promised herself. Or a dog or a cat or even a goldfish. I'll live alone forever, until I'm an old lady like Mrs. Bupp.

Rosie felt as if she lived alone already, the house was so still. But then Rosie heard a sound. She sat up, listening. It was a very small sound. And it was coming from very nearby.

52

No Way, Winky Blue!

Rosie held her breath. There it was again!
Scratch...scratch.

The sound seemed to be coming from her wastebasket.

Rosie turned on the light and tiptoed over to the wastebasket, her heart pounding. Was she imagining things, or did she see a flash of blue in the basket? Rosie pushed aside the pile of crumpled papers. The next moment, a pair of bright black eyes winked up at her.

"Chirp!" cried Winky happily.

"Aunt Maria, come quick!" yelled Rosie. "Winky's safe. Lionel didn't eat him after all!"

The next day, Mrs. Bupp came over to say good-bye. She was carrying a suitcase in one hand and a cat carrier in the other. Sticking out of the top of the cat carrier was a bald tail–Lionel's!

"I've decided to take Lionel with me," said Mrs. Bupp. "I think he'll like California."

"Good luck," said Aunt Maria.

"We'll miss you," said Rosie.

Mrs. Bupp shook hands with Aunt Maria. Then Rosie shook hands with Mrs. Bupp. She even shook Lionel's paw through the cat carrier.

"I'm sorry I thought you ate Winky for dinner," she said.

Mrs. Bupp said good-bye and turned to go. That was when Rosie noticed her hat. It was red with a cluster of feathers on top.

And the feathers were robin's egg blue.

Mrs. Bupp winked at Rosie.

"Like my hat?" she asked, patting her head. "I left it out for the thrift store, but Lionel carried it right back to me. So I decided to keep it."

Rosie smiled at Aunt Maria. So that was how the blue feather got stuck to Lionel's nose!

Before she went to bed that night, Rosie took Winky out of his cage and let him sit on her shoulder.

"Winky," she said, "I'm never going to try to turn you into a star again. From now on I'm going to love you just the way you are."

Winky hopped over and gently nipped Rosie's ear.

"I learned a lot these last few days," Rosie continued, stroking Winky's warm feathers. "I know now that you're just an ordinary parakeet."

Winky nibbled Rosie's cheek lovingly. Then he opened his beak and shouted right in her ear.

"No way!"